I0720384

A LARRY MATOYO NOVEL

LARRY BOURNE:

WHERE'S THE PHARAOH?

TAT PUBLISHING

Copyright © 2017 by Larry Matoyo
All rights reserved.
ISBN 978-1-925332-20-9

No part of this publication may be reproduced, distributed, or transmitted in any form or by any means, including photocopying, recording, or other electronic or mechanical methods, without the prior written permission of the author, except non-commercial uses permitted by copyright law.

Cover design and illustrations

by
Christopher Tupa
http://www.ctupa.com - http://www.flickr.com/tupa
Instagram: artofctupa

For permission requests, address the request to the author c/o
Permissions,
C/o TAT Publishing
PO Box 150
Glen Waverley, Victoria, 3150

www.tatpublishing.com

TABLE OF CONTENTS

PROLOGUE

Cairo, Egypt,

Renowned Egyptologist Hugh Lawson walked out of his tent with a feeling of anxiety. It had been two hours since his team stumbled upon a discovery just on the edge of the Great Pyramid of Giza, a very famous Egyptian monument that attracted tourists, scholars and even film-makers from around the world.

"Have you found it yet?" Hugh asked.

"We believe so," one of the men replied.

The man gave him a photograph of a dark, dirty chamber with hieroglyphics inscribed all over the walls. Hugh graciously took it and smiled.

"At long last."

ONE

It was a hot summer afternoon at the Cairo International Airport. The wail of an Emirates Airbus A380 pierced the air as it touched down on the runway. Jolted out of sleep by the deafening sound, Larry Bourne rubbed his eyes and waited impatiently for the seatbelt sign to flicker off before collecting his hand luggage and joining the long line of passengers already crowding to get off the plane. He had just arrived in Egypt and the heat was already unbearable.

At the age of fifteen, Larry had a brilliant problem solving mind and a vivid memory. He had bright green eyes, a buzz cut and a short, narrow chin.

Larry had taken the twenty-one-hour flight from Washington, D.C. to visit his uncle, Peter Bourne, an Egyptologist, who was supervising an archaeological dig at Giza. It had began after a small tomb was accidentally discovered by a local tourist who was taking photographs of the Great Pyramid of Giza.

The discovery had made instant headlines around the world. For a year and a half, the team were uncovering sarcophagi and Egyptian leather-bound scrolls from an ancient past.

After getting his luggage, Larry walked towards the customs. At the far left side of the arrival crowd, his uncle waited against the iron rail, casually watching news headlines flicker across the backlit screens. As he spotted his nephew, his face lit up in a beaming smile.

They greeted each other and talked over lunch at Burger King.

"So Larry, what have you been up to all these years? It's been a long time since I last saw you."

"Well not much. Just school, my family and friends," Larry replied.

Peter took out a small brown package and handed it to Larry. "I wanted to give you this on your fifteenth birthday, but an emergency caught up with me."

"What is it?"

"Open it and see."

Hurriedly, Larry cut the tape sealing the package and lifted out a "Swatch Les Adventures De Tintin". A black plastic case housed a sky blue dial with a close-up of Tintin's face and his infamous red quiff extending out from the dial onto the top of the case itself. He immediately fastened the timepiece on his wrist.

"Happy belated Birthday. As I know you love Tintin so much, I got you the watch."

"Thank you, Uncle. I love it so much."

During lunch, Peter received a call.

"Hello, this is Peter."

A voice replied on the speaker. Peter talked for some time before hanging up and suggesting they leave.

The duo arrived at the Pyramids of Giza as a nearby clock struck noon. Peter stopped at the ticket booth and showed the guards his identification badge to prove he belonged there. With a quick glance at the ID, the guards let them pass.

"How were your people allowed to work around here?" Larry asked.

"We've taken great lengths to attain this opportunity," Peter replied. "Our exploration team, led by Mr Lawson, my boss, had to be granted access from the Ministry of State for Antiquities. It was a very long process."

"I can imagine it is hard to work here with all the tourists who come here every day."

"It is hard, but the tourists don't come here. They aren't allowed to unless they have clearance."

Peter parked his black Toyota jeep with four other jeeps. There were also three quad bikes and three dirt bikes that belonged to the foundation.

Ahead of them were two large, green canvas tents. The one on the left was labelled "Discoveries" and the other "Lobby". Beside them were five smaller brown tents.

"This is our site. It's where we do all of our research and keep our equipment. We sleep in the small brown tents. You shall share one with my boss's son."

The duo headed into the "Lobby" tent where everyone inside stared at them.

"Hello guys, I'm back from the airport," Peter declared.

"Is that your nephew you were telling us about?" one of the workers asked.

"Yes. Everyone meet Larry. He is the son of my sister."

"Welcome to Cairo, Larry," a man said. He stood up immediately after the introduction. "I am Hugh Lawson, the director of this exploration team that you see in front of you."

Beside him stood two young teenagers.

"These are my children." Hugh pointed towards the teenagers. "This is my son, James Lawson and my daughter, Joan Lawson."

"Hello Larry," Joan greeted. "Welcome to Cairo, where it's incredibly hot."

"Although I'm sure you'll get used to the climate," James said.

"Thanks for the tip," Larry replied. "It's a good thing I came prepared."

"Well Larry, I'll tell you one thing," Hugh said. "You picked a good time to arrive. It's dinner time. You can just put your luggage in your tent and join us."

Larry, being led by James, went to the tent.

"So tell me Larry, where are you from?" James asked.

"Washington, D.C.," Larry replied.

"Have you ever been to Egypt before?" James asked.

"No. This is my first time."

Although Larry always dreamed of travelling around the world and seeing different sights, he had not travelled much. In fact, this was his second time in Africa, the first time being when he travelled to South Africa with his parents when he was twelve years old.

"Be sure to remind me to take you around the city to see some sights and maybe learn something new," Hugh said when they returned.

Time passed by as Larry had dinner with the team. They talked to each other and very soon, Larry got to know all of them. Each person was specialised in a certain archaeological area. They told stories from where they were from and enjoyed the meal. After finishing dinner, everyone cleaned up and separated into their tents.

Larry was in his tent with James preparing to sleep. It had been such a long day for him, and he was tired. He was just about asleep when he heard a loud scream from outside the tent. He quickly got out of his sleeping bag. James was also awake, his face filled with a sense of panic.

"What was that?" James asked.

The two shot out of their tent with their flashlights. They looked around the environment to see what made that scream. From the left of the "Lobby" tent, they saw two figures; one was being strangled by the other. The first figure looked like Tom Wood while the other was unknown. It was in a black, dusty cloak. In a split second, the unknown figure threw Tom to the ground. In an attempt to help him, the two teens rushed to his side. The unknown figure saw them coming and ran off into the darkness beyond the pyramids.

"Tom!" James rushed to his side. "We have to get him inside and give medical assistance."

The two teens assisted Tom into the "Lobby" tent. Hugh and the rest of his workers came rushing in moments later.

"What happened?" Hugh asked.

"We heard a scream from outside our tents," Peter said.

"It was Tom. He was in trouble. Someone attacked him," James explained.

Hugh got the First Aid kit and tended Tom.

"Tom, Tom! What happened?"

Tom tried to get up from the position he was in. He looked dazed but stood up and walked out of the tent, with the rest of the people following him. Slowly, he limped to a place west of the tent where there were four sarcophagi.

"Oh my God!" Hugh exclaimed.

The sarcophagi were filled with colours that shone in the light that beamed from the flashlights. The last one was left wide open.

TWO

Joan Lawson paced around the "Lobby" tent in disbelief. The fact that a mummy had awakened and escaped from its sarcophagus was still hard to process.

"It's impossible! It's just too unbelievable!" James said.

Everyone buzzed around, talking about the recent event. Tom was being cared for, yet he couldn't stop mumbling about the mummy and how it attacked him. Hugh had alerted everyone not to let their guard down - who knew what lurked around the whole area.

"Where do you think it came from?" Larry asked, standing beside James in the "Lobby" tent.

"I don't exactly know," Hugh replied. "I, myself, am confused beyond comprehension."

"The sarcophagus it came from was excavated four months ago in the pyramids. Maybe that's a clue."

"Maybe... but how would a mummy just awaken from the dead out of nowhere and attack one of my workers? It's just incomprehensible."

"Well how do we know it's a mummy?" Andrew asked. He was Tom's brother. "What if it's not a mummy but a spy from Dunn?"

"Who?" Larry asked looking lost.

"Ethan Dunn is an egocentric treasure hunter and mercenary," Hugh explained.

He paced the tent with a worried look on his face, then looked at his silver Rolex watch that was ticking over 1 AM.

"Guys, this mystery needs to be solved, but not at this

time. We all need our sleep and we can finish this tomorrow."

Within a few hours, the whole site was quiet.

"Who knows what we'll find tomorrow," Larry thought.

He had no idea.

THREE

Larry got up from his sleep at daybreak. As the morning hours of Friday arrived, the workers awoke and went on doing their activities. They gathered in the "Lobby" tent for breakfast.

Larry had his English breakfast and rushed to meet with James and Joan as they had agreed to meet after breakfast to discuss their mystery. Each of them were filled with curiosity.

"Guys I think that we should start investigating the area where the attack occurred. We could find a clue that could help us solve this mystery," Joan suggested.

The trio split up and searched the area. They examined the sand with care. It was at that moment that James saw a brownish piece of bandage.

"James, what is that?" Joan asked.

"It looks like an old bandage from the…"

"Mummy!" Larry interjected. "It can't be."

They all looked at it very closely. It looked real enough to have come from the so-called mummy.

"I don't think it's real," Joan said.

"Why not?"

"It doesn't look real. But I know a way we can see if it is." she said. "Radiocarbon dating."

"The machine is in the "Discoveries" tent. Let's go," James said.

The trio made their way to the tent. The radiocarbon dating machine had to be used by a professional so they enlisted the help off Tom's brother, Andrew Wood. They explained themselves and showed him the clue they'd found. Andrew agreed to help, however, he mentioned the process would take some time.

As the machine worked, Larry talked to Joan. Ever since he first saw her, he was astonished by her. She had small, light hazel eyes, flushed rosy cheeks, perfect white teeth, a clear complexion, fine auburn shoulder-length hair and a slim body.

"Hey," Larry greeted.

"Hey," Joan replied back. "So I'm guessing this is some crazy trip."

"It's in the top four," Larry answered. "I hope you don't mind me asking, but where's your mum? I've only seen your dad."

"Our mum is in Paris. Our parents met there, got married there and we were born there. James is only seven minutes older than me." Joan paused for a second. "However they divorced three years ago and we came to Cairo with my father."

"I'm sorry. It must've been hard for you and your brother."

"It was hard at first but we got used to it. Living with our father taught us new things like Egyptian history and culture."

A beeping sound echoed through the tent. The radiocarbon dating machine was done.

"What is it Andrew? What do the results say?"

FOUR

"The clue is fake!" Larry exclaimed.

The radiocarbon dating process showed the bandage was just a piece of a modern costume, not from an ancient mummy.

"We have to tell my father," Joan said.

As they rushed out of the tent they heard a deafening sound of rotor blades. It was a black Eurocopter EC130 helicopter hovering over the site. It slowly started descending, blowing dust and sand into every direction.

As it landed, the doors of the helicopter opened. Two men alighted in matching black outfits and made their way immediately to the "Lobby" tent.

"Who are they?" Larry asked.

"I think I know," James replied. His blue eyes concentrated firmly on them.

The trio were just about to tell Hugh about their clue but were interrupted as the two men entered.

"Hugh Lawson, I see you're still in the archaeology business," one of the men stated.

"Ethan," Hugh greeted firmly. "What are you doing here?"

"Am I not welcome here?" Ethan questioned with a sly smile.

"We all know that you're just here for the money and exposure, not for the hard work. We aren't colleagues anymore, and I'm not helping you. I know what you're after and we haven't got it."

"You know me too well, Hugh. Tell me how much?"

"How much for what?"

"How much money do you want for your find? Surely a few million can't hurt?" Ethan asked. He took out a pen and a chequebook from his pocket.

Hugh looked at Ethan with disgust. "You can't bribe me Ethan. I dedicate my time to archaeology because it has a purpose, not for the fame. Your money means nothing to me."

Ethan gave up his offer. He walked out of the tent in disappointment and looked at Hugh.

"I tried to be reasonable, Hugh, but it's clearly been some time since we were on the same level. I won't negotiate a second time." He strode off without looking back and walked towards the helicopter. As he entered, the rotor blades started rotating and the engine roared throughout the site. It took off without wasting time.

"I hope that's the last time we'll see him," Hugh said.

"Mr. Lawson," Larry called out. "If I may ask, why does he want the discovery anyway? And what is this about a treasure?"

"Larry, you know that a year prior to your arrival we had a discovery?"

"Yes."

"What you don't know is what we discovered. Come with me."

Hugh, followed by the three teens and Peter, walked to the "Discovery" tent. Inside, Hugh opened the safe and took out a small black box that was inscribed with hieroglyphics on the sides. He opened it and took out a small, worn leather-bound scroll, handing it over to Larry.

"Larry, a year ago we had speculation that there were still some uncharted chambers in the pyramid. Our infrared cameras uncovered an area in the pyramid not yet discovered. When we uncovered the chamber, we found some old documents that referred to the lost treasures of Egypt."

"Now these were all the treasures that the pharaohs had gathered and stored throughout the years. They mostly consisted of the wealthy possessions of the pharaohs such as gold bullion, priceless gems and archives."

"It is also mentioned that the treasures are in the lost tomb of Alexander the Great," James said.

"However when the Romans conquered Egypt in 30 BC, the location of the treasure was lost. Only a few managed to know where it was but weren't willing to surrender the information to the Romans. It's thought that the men who guarded the treasure made a coded map that led to the location. We have it."

"Where is it?"

"It's on the scroll you're holding. When we told the world, we obviously caught the attention of archaeologists and also treasure hunters - including Ethan Dunn. Knowing Ethan, he will stop at nothing to get his hands on that treasure."

Larry handed the scroll back to Hugh who then placed it back in its box. He placed the box back in the safe and locked it.

Suddenly Larry remembered why they were in the tent in the first place - the piece of bandage.

"Mr. Lawson, before you go, we need to show you this." He took the bandage and handed it to Hugh.

"What is this?"

"It's a bandage we found at the location where Tom was attacked last night. At first we thought it belonged to the mummy Tom talked about but then we carbon-dated it and realised it was a fake. It was just a piece from a costume."

Hugh examined it closely. "Do you suppose this is sabotage?"

"Yes."

"And we think it's Ethan Dunn," Joan said.

FIVE

The day ended with the whole team gathering for dinner in the "Lobby" tent during the evening. Everyone was present, including Tom who had recovered from his bruises. It had been a bad day for the team. The bad news was the threat from Ethan Dunn. And the news was about to get worse.

Joan had gone into her tent to read her novel in her sleeping bag. Hugh, together with Peter and some other members were in "Discoveries" tent discussing their plans for the expedition. They planned to go further into the pyramids in the hopes of finding new discoveries. The whole site was quiet, the only sound was from Larry and James's tent. They had been talking about different topics that came into their minds.

By midnight they were both tired and started dozing off. Suddenly, Larry awoke to a sound that startled him - footsteps. Who could be outside at this time? A surge of fear and adrenaline rushed through him. What if it was the intruder from yesterday? Had they returned to cause trouble again? Then he saw a silhouette passing his tent. Panic gripped him. He wanted to shout and alert everyone about them but what if he was attacked? Slowly without making a sound, Larry got out of his sleeping bag and peeped outside to see who the silhouette was. Upon seeing who it was, he breathed a huge sigh of relief. It was just Tom Wood. But what was he doing outside at this hour of night?

Tom, keen on making no noise, walked slowly towards the "Lobby" tent. He stopped and stood for a few minutes. He was waiting for someone. He was joined by someone else, his brother, Andrew.

"Where is he?" Andrew asked his brother.

"He'll be here soon. He said he would be."

Larry was confused. Who was this person they were waiting for? His question was answered when out of the dark, a third figure appeared. Larry could not believe his eyes. He thought it must've been a dream - Tom and Andrew were joined by Ethan.

"What have you got for me boys?" Ethan asked with a coy smile.

"Boss, we know where the map is. It's in the safe," Andrew answered.

"In a safe?"

"Yes. It's a four-digit pass code safe."

"How interesting. I don't suppose you know this code?"

"Uh, not just yet."

"Damn!" Ethan cursed. Then an idea came into his mind. "We could make him hand over the map."

"How?" Tom asked puzzled.

"A deal. I'm sure he can trade it over for something he considers valuable. Perhaps a close thing, like a family member."

"He has two children. One of them sleeps alone," Andrew said.

Larry was shocked and a wave of fear and panic surged through him again. They were talking about Joan - she was not sharing her tent with anyone.

"Where is her tent?" Ethan asked. The three of them set off to carry out their devious plan.

Without wasting time, Larry tried waking James, but his friend was sound asleep. He was just about to rush out and confront them himself, but realised he may not be able to save Joan in time. There were three of them and they could have weapons. Larry only had was his Swiss pocket knife. He needed James's help. Furiously shaking his friend until James opened his eyes in fright, Larry explained to him everything he had heard between the three men and their devious plan. James was now fully awake.

"Let's not waste time. Come on!"

They rushed towards Joan's tent. Without thinking, the boys threw the canvas wall aside and bumped straight into Tom and Andrew, who turned around and instantly had the boys pinned to the ground.

"Boss," Tom called out to Ethan. "You better hurry up. We have some young company."

Joan heard the scuffle and woke to realise she was not alone in her tent. She wanted to scream for help but Ethan's arm was firmly placed on her mouth to prevent her from making a sound. She panicked and started thrashing about to escape. It was no use. Ethan placed a handkerchief over her mouth that smelt bitter and acidic. Catching sight of Larry and James, she attempted to release herself from Ethan's iron grip, but her strength was lost and the world went black.

Without wasting time, Ethan pushed Joan out of the tent and ran into the darkness beyond while the boys struggled to escape.

"He's getting away!" Larry shouted to James. They were still struggling to get up but Tom and Andrew were not going to let them go so easily. Each received a short, quick punch to the head and blacked out.

SIX

Larry awoke slowly. His skull ached. As his vision finally began to clear, he realised it was morning. He was on a bed. Beside him was James. They were in the "Lobby" tent.

The back of Larry's head throbbed, a gnawing pain. Gingerly, he reached up with his free arm and touched his scalp, trying to locate the source of his headache. Beneath his matted hair, he found a huge lump, pain searing through his mind.

Three people were standing beside them. Hugh and Peter stood to his right. They were talking to a tall, stout man holding a manila folder. They became startled when they saw Larry coming to.

"Larry, oh my God!" Peter exclaimed. "What happened to you two?"

"Joan," Larry managed. "She...she's gone."

Hugh pushed aside Peter. "What happened? Where is my daughter?"

Larry managed to answer two words. "Ethan Dunn."

"I am Detective Inspector Xavier Peters. Do you remember what happened before you passed out, son?"

"Yes," Larry replied groggily. He explained to them everything that happened before Joan's kidnapping.

James awoke a few minutes later. He recalled last night's events and the horrible truth. Joan was kidnapped by Ethan. The whole site was in grief.

"I can't believe Tom and Andrew betrayed us. It seems they were spies," Peter said.

"Detective, will you be able to find my sister?" James asked.

"I will do my best. I'm advising you to remain calm while we're on the case. We're doing the best we can," Detective Peters replied.

"How do we know you'll find her?" James asked. "It might take a long time. He could be gone with no trace."

A long silence followed after James spoke. What if it was true? They were all worried. There was a laptop on the wooden table in the middle of them. Suddenly it flickered on. The screen showed a dark and dirty basement. In the middle was the screen was a face. A very familiar face.

"You!" Larry exclaimed. "You foul son of a..."

"Call me whatever you want! I still have someone here you value," Ethan interrupted.

The screen then turned to about 90 degrees and showed her. There was Joan. She was tied up in the chair with a gag in her mouth. She made muffled sounds. There was fear in her eyes.

"Listen to me. I asked for the treasure and you refused. I'm giving you another deal, give me the treasure and she walks away. I'm giving you three days or you'll never see her again."

The laptop screen turned black. Everyone around it was quiet, fear had gripped them. They had three days to save Joan.

Detective Xavier Peters's cell rang. He received the call and talked for a few seconds before hanging up.

"Mr. Lawson, leave this case to me. I will stop at nothing to find your daughter."

SEVEN

Three hours had passed since Ethan's threat was declared. The whole site had one thing on their mind - rescuing Joan. They had to find the treasure, and the scroll had the only way to find its location.

Hugh hurried to the "Discoveries" tent. Peter saw him and followed along with Larry and James. Upon arriving at the tent, he opened the safe and took out the box. He opened it and took out the scroll.

"Hugh, what are you up to?" Peter asked.

"I think this may help us get back my daughter," Hugh replied firmly.

With a soft touch, he opened it. It wasn't the complete map, but rather a clue. There were two phrases written in hieroglyphics. Hugh translated:

"From Cheops's earthly tomb the path unfolds
Across Egypt the mystic locations foretold."

"Why couldn't the ancient Egyptians just say where the treasure is and how to get there? Instead we are facing a major crisis and all we have are complex riddles," Larry complained.

"You're right about that Larry," James continued. "The only phrase I understand is 'Cheops's earthly tomb'. I think it is talking about the Great Pyramid of Giza. That is where Cheops, one of the earliest pharaohs is buried."

"Are you suggesting the first clue to finding the treasure is in the pyramid?" Larry asked. "If so, why are we still standing here?"

"No! No one is going into the pyramid. It isn't safe down

there," Hugh exclaimed.

"Dad, we have to!" James replied. "It's the only way we can save Joan."

"I agree," Peter said. "We have three days to find her and we cannot just waste precious time arguing about it."

"I still don't agree. It's bad enough my daughter is gone. I'm not going to risk your lives as well. I'm the head of this expedition so I decide what to do. End of discussion."

"And what about Joan?" James asked. "We have a chance to save her!"

"The police will take care of it!"

"How do we know that? She could be anywhere in the world right now and the police don't know about this clue!"

"James, enough of this! I have made my final decision about it and none of you are going into that pyramid! End of discussion!"

No one could disagree with Hugh's final decision. He closed the scroll and locked it back in the safe. Everyone else walked out of the tent in disappointment.

Night time arrived. Everyone was glum during dinner. The usual chatter was replaced by silence. After dinner, everyone separated into their tents. As Larry was going to his tent, someone yanked him from behind and covered his mouth from making noise. Larry panicked and immediately took action. He elbow punched the person and stepped on him. The person made a cry of pain. Larry turned around - the person was none other than James.

"James, what was that for?"

"Oh don't worry about me. I'm fine," James sarcastically replied, but he was definitely going to get a bruise from that punch.

"Why would you do that?"

"Because I thought it would be fun," James sarcastically replied again. "I needed your attention."

"Then why didn't you just call me?"

"I didn't want anyone hearing what I'm about to ask you."

"What do you want?"

"I need your help. You and I both know that the scroll is our only way to save Joan. My dad won't help much, so I need you. Are you willing to come with me on this mystery?"

Larry though for a while. It was true that the scroll was the clue they needed to find the treasure and save Joan. The only question was what could go wrong? He had been on a number of small mysteries but this was something else.

"Well, are you with me?" James said reeling Larry from his thoughts. "Are you going to help?"

"Yes."

"Great. We'll need some equipment first and go."

"What equipment?"

"Rope, a map, a compass and other supplies."

"And how are we going to get the scroll? Isn't it in a safe?"

"Earlier today I watched and memorized the pass-code when he was opening it."

"Are you sure about this plan?" Larry once again asked.

"Do you want to save Joan or not?" James asked firmly.

"I do."

"Good. We'll carry out the plan."

A few minutes later the teens had all their equipment. James had managed to sneak into the "Discoveries" tent and opened the safe without alerting anyone. He took the scroll from the box and returned it as it was. From there, he met with Larry who had managed to get some necessary items in his pockets. When no one was looking, they got out of their tent and headed for the pyramid. James shone his torch at Larry.

"Are you sure you're ready for this?"

Larry paused for a few seconds to consider the question. Seriously. This wasn't a game after all. He could get hurt, and so could his friend. He looked at his watch and remembered how he was inspired by Tintin, not only to go out for adventures, but to help people in need.

"Yes. Let's go save Joan."

EIGHT

Joan awoke and looked around. She was alone in a dark room. Above, the only source of light was an old fashioned bulb on a bare white wire and its switch was nowhere to be seen. There was a wooden door to her left. In front of her was a small wooden table with a laptop on it.

Earlier that day, she had seen her family on that screen. They were terrified, with fear in their eyes. The same fear had gripped her. She tried to move her hands but they were bound tightly to the chair and so were her legs. She tried to speak but no sound came out. She was gagged as well.

Suddenly the door opened and Ethan came in. He turned on the light that filled the room with brightness, walked directly to Joan and removed the gag.

"I see you're awake," Ethan said.

"Where are we?" Joan asked firmly.

"Somewhere that you can't know."

"What do you want with me?"

"You, my dear Joan, are going to force your father to hand me the treasure. Besides he wouldn't want to see his daughter face a horrible fate."

"You will not get away with this. My family will find me and put you in jail."

Ethan smiled and replied. "We shall see."

He then put the gag back in her mouth as she resisted and walked to the exit.

There in the darkness, Joan looked for a way she could get out. Then she had an idea. The laptop.

NINE

Larry gazed in wonder at the massive stones of the tourist entrance to the pyramid. Only a handful of people had been inside the pyramid and he was about to be one of them. With their flashlights in hand, they walked into the darkness.

"So what are we looking for exactly?" Larry asked.
James took out the scroll from his pocket and read it.
"From Cheops's earthly tomb the path unfolds
Across Egypt the mystic locations are foretold.
"I'm guessing something to do with Cheops's tomb. From there maybe we'll find the next clue."
"Alright, but where exactly is Cheops's tomb?"

James took out a small black leather journal and opened past a few pages. He then stopped and observed what looked like a map and some instructions on the page. Larry caught a glimpse of the map and understood the situation.

"According to my dad's journal, Cheops's tomb is deep beneath the pyramid."

"How did he know where he is buried?"

"They found some documents depicting where Cheops was buried. He must have translated and copied them into his journal. They were thinking of coming down here but we're stopped by funding and my dad wasn't sure he was willing to disturb the resting place of Cheops for fame."

They continued their way into the darkness. After a few minutes of walking downwards, the teens arrived at an unfinished chamber directly under the pyramid. It was a dead end.

"What now?" Larry asked.

Without wasting time, James opened the journal to the page with the map and read the instructions that were written down by his father.

"There is a secret passage right here that will lead us even deeper in the pyramid. We just have to find it." James then turned the journal towards Larry and showed him the page. Larry's attention was caught by a series of four Egyptian symbols.

"We have to find the symbols in order," James continued. "By finding these symbols..."

"The passage will open," Larry interrupted James. "I get it."

Without wasting time the teens began their search. Using his sleuthing skills, Larry scanned the wall ahead of him.

There were no symbols on the wall. He took a step back and thought for a while. Then a thought struck him. He scanned the dusty floor. He rubbed sand until he found something. It looked like a part of one of the symbols he had seen.

"James, I think I found..."

In a flash, James came beside him. "What is it?"

Larry showed him the clue and kept on rubbing sand until he saw the full thing. It looked exactly like one of the symbols on the page.

"Great job. We just to find the other three symbols and the passage will be revealed."

"I wonder..." Larry continued rubbing sand at the symbol. As he did he caught a peculiar sight to the left end of the first uncovered symbol. He shifted his position to the sight that caught his eye and started rubbing sand from the place. Slowly, Larry uncovered another symbol. He was just about to inform James when his name was called out.

"Did you find anything?" Larry asked.

"I found two symbols. What about you?"

"I also found another symbol. I guess we found all four of them."

James opened the page and instructed Larry on what to do. He started by pressing the two symbols he had found followed by Larry, who pressed the two symbols he had found in order. Nothing. Then a loud thud was heard from the other side. A crack became visible from the wall. Slowly the crack moved around the wall and formed a circular shape. Carefully, James moved towards the shape and gently applied pressure on it. As he did, the shape moved backwards and fell into the next section. Larry and James saw beyond the circular doorway. There was a stone stairway that led deep down in the pyramid.

"Down we go," Larry said.

Time passed by as the teens walked through the ancient stairway that led deep within the colossal monument. Later onwards the boys were greeted by platforms of wood that looked like a chess board. On the platforms of wood were more hieroglyphics. They did not make any sense to Larry. He was just about to walk over one of them when he was pulled back by James.

"Watch out Larry. This is a trap."

"How do you know?"

James picked up a small rock from the dusty floor, motioned Larry to stand back and threw it to the platforms. It landed on one of them and immediately the platform exploded. The echo roared across the whole room and passages and wooden splinters flew all over. Larry gasped.

"There is a page in the journal that explains about the traps set up in the pyramid to stop thieves. I found the details about this trap. It is pressure sensitive and explodes if you step on the wrong platform," James explained.

He took out the journal and opened a few pages. He stopped at a page and showed it to Larry. On the page were the same symbols as on the platforms. Some were crossed out.

"Do you see these symbols?" James asked pointing at the crossed out symbols. "We must avoid these symbols on the platform to get across. One step on the wrong platforms would be fatal."

Step by step, the teens moved through the platforms, being careful not to step on the wrong ones. One false move could mean disaster. They were just about to make it across, when Larry lost his balance and missed a step. A few inches of his left foot stepped on the wrong platform. He panicked. Without taking a glance ahead, the boys rushed across, not caring if they were right or wrong. The platforms exploded. The echo of the blast blared around and wooden splinters and dust particles flew over. The blast wave shook the boys off their feet just as they made it across. They slowly got up with dust on their clothes and looked back. The platforms had been replaced with a huge gap. It seemed endless due to the darkness within. Two seconds later, they heard the faint thud of the wood as it crashed below.

The passage continued into the darkness. The teens moved on. After minutes of walking in the ancient passage filled with cobwebs, the teens arrived at some sort of doorway. It was made of stone. On the door were four circles arranged in a square. A foot from the door was a hole in the stone. The hole was surrounded by a square carved in the stone.

The boys looked closely at the door. "Is this another trap?" Larry asked.

James opened the journal at scanned past the pages. "I don't know. Nothing is mentioned about this door in the journal."

"What if this is not a trap?" Larry asked again. His hand slowly reached at the edge. James watched him and stopped his hand.

"I still think this is a trap. We don't know what might happen and we are far away from help."

"You are right, but we are doing this for your sister. We have to take the risk or else we won't find her," Larry said, trying to sound confident but he still had doubts.

James let Larry's hand slip from his grip and watched as Larry placed his hand in the hole. His face was filled with fear. What would happen next?

Larry felt a wooden lever in the hole. He pulled it and waited to see what would happen next.

Suddenly, the stone door opened.

TEN

The boys glanced at the huge, ancient room ahead of them. It was dark and the only light inside was the fluorescent light coming from the flashlights of the boys. On the walls of the room were brass bowls that had what seemed like charcoal in them.

"Let's light these up," Larry said. "We could see much better."

James took out a lighter from his shirt pocket. He lit the six charcoal bowls with fire. The light made the room clearer. The walls were decorated with paintings and hieroglyphics. The paintings were wearing out, except for some parts that were embedded with hieroglyphics. The floor was dusty, clearly indicating that no one had been in there for a very long time. At the ceiling of the room was a huge painting of an Egyptian pharaoh and under the painting directly in the centre was a sarcophagus. It glinted in the light due to the gold and different colours on it. The sarcophagus was placed above a golden altar that had five jars decorated with hieroglyphics. At the end of the room was a small black box inscribed with hieroglyphics on the sides. It was placed on a thick wooden stand.

"Is this..." Larry paused in disbelief. "Is this Cheops's sarcophagus?"

James couldn't believe what he was seeing. For years, Egyptologists had been trying to find his tomb but had no luck, yet here they were, just two teenagers, standing right in front of it. They both felt a feeling of pride. However the feeling soon disappeared at the thought of his sister. She would have been astounded to see this.

Larry paid attention to the small box behind the sarcophagus. It looked like the one Hugh had showed him, which contained the scroll. A thought came into his mind. He looked at James and knew that he also had the same thought.

"This is the next clue." Larry said. "It has to be."

"Open it," James said anxiously. "What is the next clue?"

Larry opened the box. It had the exact layout as the first one. He took out the scroll and opened it. And just like the first one, there were phrases written on it in hieroglyphics. Larry could not understand the meaning and gave it to James who then translated with the guide of the journal.

"Sun by day, fire by night,
The lighthouse shines the way,
It stands high in Alexandria."

ELEVEN

It was 3 AM. Joan had been trying to get herself to the laptop to contact someone for help. She managed to get closer to the laptop but still faced a challenge. The ropes were tightly bound around her hands and feet. She looked around the room for something that could cut the ropes. She could feel her back pocket. Something was in it.

She put her hand into the pocket while trying to ignore the coarse grip of the ropes that hurt her. She took out a pocket knife. She smiled at Ethan's mistake - he didn't search her pockets. Without hesitating she cut the ropes and felt blood rushing through her veins. She sat in front of the laptop. Her excitement turned to disappointment when she realized Ethan had a password.

Surely, no matter how smart he was, his memory wasn't so great – this had to be easy. What was the easiest four-letter word Ethan would remember? His last name! She typed in "Dunn". It was a success. She opened her e-mail and contacted her father.

Dear Dad,
I'm fine, but I don't know where I am or how long I have until something worse happens to me. Please help me.
Joan.

She turned off and closed the laptop, binding her ropes again in the hopes that Ethan wouldn't catch on to her.

TWELVE

"Alexandria! How are we going to get there?" Larry asked surprised. He hadn't planned to travel to Alexandria.

"The phrases point to Alexandria," James replied. "We have to go there and find the next clue. And the good thing is we have a specific point to go. The Citadel of Qaitbay."

"I thought the clue said the Lighthouse of Alexandria not..."

"The Lighthouse of Alexandria was destroyed in an earthquake years ago. Where it was built stands the Citadel of Qaitbay. In fact, some of the actual bricks that belonged to the lighthouse were used to build the fortress."

James continued to read from his guide book:

"Located 129 miles from Cairo, Alexandria is the second largest city and a major economic centre in Egypt. It sits along the Mediterranean Sea and known to attract tourists across the world. Tourists travelled here to see monuments and museums like the Bibliotheca Alexandrina and Pompey's Pillar.

The Citadel of Qaitbay is a 15th-century defensive fortress built upon the ruins of the Lighthouse of Alexandria. Established in 1477 AD by Sultan Al-Ashraf Sayf al-Din Qa'it Bay, the Citadel is situated on the eastern side of the northern tip of Pharos Island at the mouth of the Eastern Harbour."

"How are we going to get there exactly?" Larry asked again.

James took out his phone. He was able to get a better signal since he was out of the pyramid. They had taken another tunnel within the pyramid that had led them to their current location, outside the Sphinx. After a few minutes of searching the Internet, James had found a way.

"We can take the train. It's the fastest mode rather than the bus."

Larry was confused. "What makes you think your father is going to allow us to go to Alexandria? He didn't want us to solve this mystery in the first place."

"Who said anything about telling my father about Alexandria? He probably won't allow us and will be furious that we disobeyed him and went into the pyramids. We are on our own."

"What is your plan?"

"We are going to "borrow" some money from my dad's wallet and go to Alexandria on our own. We'll find this treasure and save my sister."

James was serious. He was not going to give up easily and let his sister meet her end. He was determined to rescue her. Larry could see he was serious and reluctantly agreed.

"The train that leaves at 6 AM will do. We just need the money."

Larry checked his watch. It was 23.49. He was exhausted. Together with James, he walked back to the site.

The "Lobby" tent was occupied by Hugh and Peter. Peter was tired while Hugh continuously made telephone calls. The police had contacted him stating there was still no sign of his daughter. Larry and James sneaked their way to Hugh's tent. While Larry waited outside. James entered the tent and looked through his father's personal belongings. He later came out disappointment. He couldn't find it. He thought for a while and came up with an idea.

"I'll get it later. For now we have to sleep. We'll get up at 4 AM."

"Good idea."

The teens made their way to their tent and got some sleep. They needed all the energy they could get for the next day.

Meanwhile, Hugh was still on the phone and using his laptop. Earlier he had received an e-mail from Joan, a sign that she was still alive. He was on the phone with Detective Inspector Xavier Peters.

"Are you able to trace where the e-mail was sent from?" Hugh asked firmly.

"Don't worry Mr. Lawson. We will find her," Xavier replied.

THIRTEEN

Larry awoke suddenly. He heard a beeping sound emitting from the alarm clock. He turned it off and looked at the time. As planned the alarm had rang at 4 AM. He woke James up and immediately prepared himself. James did the same.

Afterwards he silently and cautiously walked to Hugh's tent, searching for his father's wallet. Larry, standing outside the tent, advised James to look in pockets of the clothes he wore yesterday. He saw his father's trousers right next to his sleeping bag and searched them. Success. He found Hugh's wallet and opened it. There were his cards and notes. He took out 100 Egyptian pounds and returned the wallet. He quickly got out and left a note for Hugh.

"Alright, I have the money. Let's go."

Larry checked his watch. It was just after 4:30 AM. "We have an hour and a half left before the train leaves."

"We can catch the 6 AM train at Ramses Station and get to Alexandria by 9:45 AM."

They took their small rucksacks filled with important equipment and left the site with a dirt bike belonging to the team. At the ticket booth, they found the guard still asleep on his leather chair. They opened the gate themselves, gunned the bike engine and left.

Security guard Gustavo Castillo awoke suddenly from his sleep. He was awaken by the sound of a bike engine nearby. He rubbed his eyes and looked outside the booth. The gate was wide open. He checked his security camera and noticed two boys on a dirt bike, leaving the site.

FOURTEEN

The sound of the telephone roused Hugh Lawson from his sleep. He rolled over and checked his watch: 5:06 AM. Unnerved, he sat up in his sleeping bag and picked up the receiver.

"Mr. Lawson, Security guard Gustavo Castillo here. We've got a problem."

"What is it?" Hugh moaned.

"It's about your son."

Hugh sat bolt upright, now fully awake. "What is it?"

"He and that other teenager who arrived recently took one of the dirt bikes."

"Do you know where they are going?" Hugh asked firmly.

"I have no clue."

Hugh left the telephone and hurried to James's tent. Upon arriving, he didn't find either of the boys. Then, his eyes gazed at a folded paper on James's sleeping bag. He took it and read what was written on it.

Dear Dad,

We have gone to the Citadel of Qaitbay to show Larry the sights of Egypt. Also while we're there, we'll find Joan. Don't worry about us.

James.

P.S. We may have borrowed some money too. I'll pay you back when I can.

Without hesitation, Hugh should have known his son wouldn't take no for an answer, especially when it concerned his twin sister. He took his rucksack and started to pack the necessities.

"Good morning Hugh," Peter greeted.

"Peter, hurry up and get dressed," Hugh said.

Peter looked confused. "Why? What is going on?"

"We're going to Alexandria."

FIFTEEN

The eerie basement where Joan was held had two ways out. The first way was through the door, but it was locked shut. The other way was the window, but it was too high for her to reach. She looked around the empty room and the only thing that could help her reach the window was the table that the laptop was placed on.

Although the table looked heavy, Joan could still move it. With great determination she heaved it towards the window and climbed it. It was still dark outside except for the well-lit up streets. She looked at her watch. It was almost 6 AM. She opened the small window and a rush of cold air hit her face as her eyes scanned the streets. As she looked outside she realised her escape was not going to be easy.

The room she was in was just below ground level in the Old City. She could see the feet of occasional passers-by, pacing the sidewalk. Locking her elbows, she jumped from the table and heaved herself through the small gap, lying low to protect her head. Squeezing through the dirty window, she grabbed the bars of a shaky metal grate, holding it to give her that extra leverage to get out. The echo of the metal being hit by her force echoed. She hoped Ethan and his goons did not hear it. She pulled herself over the ledge and darted through the street without turning back.

Ethan was woken by the faint ringing of metal. He stood up and opened the window to see what it was. Looking down at the street, he could see an outline of a girl under a nearby streetlight, running through the shadows. Immediately he walked to the room he had locked Joan in. He unlocked the door - there was the laptop, the chair and the table, a pile of rope on the floor but no sign of Joan. The window was wide open.

Ethan sprinted out of the room while angrily shouting to his agents who were still asleep.

"She escaped through the window! Get up, we have to stop her!"

No one was roused by him. He ignored them, opened the door and rushed downstairs after Joan.

But she was too fast, sprinting as fast as she could for the city bus.

Ethan reached the bus stop seconds before the bus pulled out from the curb. Then, he saw her through one of the windows just before the bus rounded a corner and disappeared from him. Ethan stood on the wide avenue looking for a way to catch up to her before it was too late. He could not go back to the flat and take his SUV because by then, Joan would have been long gone to the police.

Across the street, he eyed an old Vespa 250 motorcycle on the sidewalk. He raced towards it and tried to kick-start the Vespa but it coughed and died. He rammed his foot on the starter again. The little bike sprang to life. She could run but she couldn't hide!

SIXTEEN

Opened in 1856, the Ramses Railway Station is the main railway station of Cairo. Larry and James parked their dirt bike just outside Ramses Square and walked inside the train station. Larry looked at his watch again: 5:45 AM. They marched past the ticket office and headed straight for the ticket machine. After purchasing their tickets they headed towards the train and boarded it. Within a few minutes, the engines started and the train left the station.

Half an hour later, Hugh Lawson arrived at the train station. He killed the engine of the jeep and got out. He looked around the place, hoping to get a lead on his son. Then, he caught a glimpse of a familiar dirt bike. He motioned for Peter to look at it. They instantly knew it - but there was no sign of James or Larry.

Hugh and Peter rushed inside the train station. Upon arriving they both looked at the overhead screen showing the arrivals and departures. The train to Alexandria had left over half an hour ago.

"We missed the train, Hugh," Peter said in a disappointed tone.

Hugh looked again at the overhead screen. "We have another chance. The next train to Alexandria leaves at 8 AM."

Far away from the train station, Ethan Dunn paced the old Vespa 250 motorcycle after the bus. He was not going to give up easily. The bus would eventually stop and when it did, he would get Joan back.

On the bus, Joan sat still hoping she was safely away from Ethan. Her plan was to go to the nearest police station when it arrived in Cairo, alerting them about Ethan Dunn's devious plan and hopefully reuniting her with her family. Ethan's hopes were renewed when the bus reached its final stop. Joan came out of the bus being the last passenger. Catching sight of her, Ethan moved closer but maintained his distance, making sure not to alert her. He moved closer and closer. She was within his grasp.

Joan felt a cold hand on her shoulder. Startled, she turned to see Ethan. He pulled her closer and put his arm around her. Then, she felt a small sharpness on her back. Ethan held a small pen knife, concealed by his motorcycle gloves.

"If you make any attempt to run missy, I'll draw a pretty picture on your back with my knife," Ethan said in a low voice. "Move."

SEVENTEEN

The morning sun glinted off the sleek roof of Egypt's high-velocity train as it raced northward to Alexandria. Despite travelling away from Cairo at 174 miles per hour, the train made almost no noise, its soft repetitive clicking and gentle swaying motion having an almost soothing effect on those who rode it.

Now, aboard the high-speed train, Larry and James were seated on two of the leather seats, ravenously eating an assortment of sandwiches and mineral water. An hour after the train left Ramses Railway Station, James's phone buzzed to life. He had a message and it was from his father. Despite knowing his father was worried, James still had hope that they could find his sister in time – even though they only had one day left.

Larry, on the other hand, had no idea what was going to happen but he was willing to help James. His plan was to visit his uncle for his vacation, but instead he was on a train bound for Alexandria. But he did not care. In two hours, they would step into Alexandria.

Far away from them, Detective Peters was rushing towards Hugh and Peter at the Ramses Station. There were now two problems facing them. Joan was still missing and now James and Larry had run away.

"Mr. Lawson, do you know where your son went?"

"Alexandria," Hugh replied.

"How was he able to get a train ticket?"

"He found my wallet and took some cash with him. James is smart but spontaneous, I can only think they went to find Joan themselves."

Detective Peters turned to his fellow policemen.

"What's the plan?"

"We'll search for Ethan Dunn – hopefully we can find him and force him to tell us where he's keeping the young girl. We've got a lead to Cairo. As for the boys, sir, we're unsure as to where they could be."

"James would certainly go after Joan, but he said he was going to the Citadel of Qaitbay in Alexandria," Hugh interrupted. "I can't think why he would go there instead of looking for her in the capital though. Peter and I will follow them to Alexandria, hopefully you can find my daughter."

Detective Peters looked at the overhead screen, flickering between destinations.

"Right, I'll call the police chief in Cairo and ask them to send out an urgent message to their squads. My men will take the next train there in ten minutes. Hugh, our train leaves in five."

Joan Lawson's mind raced to think of a way out of the problem. She was in Ethan's clutches again and time was running out. They were still at the bus station, apparently waiting for someone. Then, a black jeep stopped in front of them. Ethan and Joan walked and entered the jeep. In seconds, it whisked off into the streets. The next seconds for Joan were a blur. She felt a sharp pain on her neck and slowly her vision started to blur. Then everything went black.

EIGHTEEN

Larry stepped out of the silver train at the El Raml train station, followed by James. From a distance they heard the sound of crashing waves and smelt the salty air from the turgid waters of the Mediterranean Sea. They had arrived at Alexandria but their mission was far from over. The boys quickly headed out of the train station and waved down a taxi.

"Where to?" the taxi driver asked.

"The Lighthouse of Alexandria," James replied.

"Where?" the driver looked puzzled.

"The Citadel of Qaitbay," Larry said.

After mindless minutes of overtaking and veering past traffic, the taxi stopped at the entrance to the monument.

The boys now stood outside the colossal fortress with the Egyptian flag flying at the top.

"What are we looking for exactly?" Larry asked.

"I don't know," James replied. The scroll says:

'Sun by day, fire by night,
The lighthouse shines the way,
It stands high in Alexandria.'

"Sun by day, fire by night, the lighthouse shines the way. What could that mean?" Larry thought. The lighthouse was a guide to sailors who were coming and going from the ports during the day and night.

At the top of the lighthouse was the lantern which was lit with fire as a guiding beacon. Was the lantern the object they had to find?

"Could it be the lantern that was at the top of the lighthouse?"

"It could be but the lantern was never found after the earthquake destroyed the lighthouse," James replied. "We are going to have to search for it."

The boys got past the gateway, heading straight for the main tower past the courtyard of the citadel entered through the main wooden door. Inside the ancient hallway, there were four doorways leading to the different floors of the fortress.

"Why don't we split up?" Larry suggested. "We could cover more ground that way."

"Good idea," James replied. "I will search the first floor while you go to the ground floor. Be careful."

"You too."

James ran up the ancient stairway while Larry raced across the patterned floor of the citadel. Minutes passed by as the duo searched the chambers and walls. The boys met back at the stairway to the first floor.

"Did you find anything?" James asked.

"Yes. I think I know where the lantern is," Larry replied. "There was a cross vault where the sultan sat and watched the ships that came in to the port. There could be a clue in that room."

"Where is that room?"

"On the third floor of the fortress."

In no time, the duo ran up the stairs to the third floor, past the tourists that were going up and down the stairway. The third floor contained several small rooms separated by similar pathways. The duo found the sultan's room in no time, defined by a large, white and gray marble seat.

"My guess is there is a clue around the seat."

The seat was not allowed to be touched but seeing there was no one to stop them, Larry moved closer and began his examination. He touched the cresting of the seat and gently moved his hand across it. Then a piece of the marble sunk into the chair. A loud thud echoed across the room.

"What was that?" James asked.

Larry looked around the room to identify the source of the sound. Then the back of the seat opened and revealed an ancient safe. Larry took out the safe and examined it. It was a wooden safe with a locking system like the one that is currently used today for pin tumbler locks. But where was the key? Larry looked at the chair again, at the fine engraved symbols along its arms and across its back. Upon closer inspection, a flower in the design was askew, just slightly different to its counterpart on the adjacent arm. Touching the embellishment, he felt the cold curve of metal – the key was hidden in the middle of the flower! He took the key, inserted it into the keyhole and opened it. Inside the safe was nothing but a small scroll.

"James, I found another scroll."

James leaned closer. "What does this one say?"

"The path of the treasure is laid,
It lies beneath the harbour,
Let the key guide thee on thy quest."

NINETEEN

Ethan Dunn took a long sip from his canned beer. He turned on his laptop to send Hugh another threat, yet it seemed his rival had already given up in an e-mail:

Ethan,
I have found what you are looking for. Meet me in Alexandria.
Hugh.

Ethan grinned and put down his bottle of beer.

"Men, we're going to Alexandria. Grab the girl and let's go."

On the express train headed for Alexandria, Hugh shut down his laptop and drank his coffee. Peter sat next to him while opposite of him was Detective Xavier.

"Do you think this plan will work?" Hugh asked.

"I am certain," Detective Xavier replied. His plan was now in motion.

The train started to slow down as it reached its destination, El Raml train station. The Mediterranean Sea came into view as the train stopped at last. The three men walked out of the train and the salty air struck them. Hugh was familiar to this smell and the sights around him. An old memory jogged back into his mind. He had spent a vacation in Alexandria with his wife before they divorced. But that didn't matter now - he was here to save his children. He emerged from the blissful memory and back into the depressing present.

TWENTY

Larry and James walked down the deserted staircase to the ground floor. They walked across the patterned floor and outside the wooden door. Up ahead, a young male guide was together with a group of people teaching them the history of the fortress.

"Excuse me sir," Larry interrupted, "Is there any path beneath the fortress?"

The guide thought for a while and answered Larry. "Actually, I'm sorry...there are no paths open to the public."

"Not one?"

The docent eyed them strangely. "There was an old path used by sailors under one of the turrets. But since the earthquake, it has been inaccessible."

The boys tried to look disappointed, but this wasn't going to stop them.

Heading towards the west tower, Larry and James sneaked behind the guard rail and into the darkness behind a pillar. Waiting for a tour group to walk past the door, the boys shut the heavy wooden door and slid the bolt home.

Larry and James began to examine the walls for a clue. Nothing. James took out the poem again and read for a hint.

The path of the treasure is laid,

It lies beneath the harbour,

Let the key guide thee on thy quest.

"Larry do you still have the key?" James asked.

Larry took out the key from his pocket and tossed it to James. He took out his glow stick from his rucksack and lit it up. Under the fluorescent light, he carefully examined the old key.

"Is there any clue on the key?" Larry asked.

"No. Perhaps there is a keyhole somewhere which this key opens?"

James shone the flashlight around the walls. Then Larry saw something out of the corner of his eye. Something glinted in the shadows. Larry shone the flashlight straight at the point that glinted. He slowly proceeded to the wall.

"Eureka!" Larry exclaimed. "James get over here with the key."

James proceeded to Larry to see what he discovered. Upon seeing the discovery, he too was astonished.

TWENTY-ONE

Peter, Hugh and Detective Xavier arrived at the El Raml Police Department. Detective Xavier led the group towards the secretary.

"Good afternoon sir," the secretary greeted. "How may I help you?"

"We have three missing children. My daughter Joan Lawson is being held hostage by Ethan Dunn – at least we think it's him. My son James and his friend Larry Bourne ran off to try and save her."

The secretary immediately stood up from her leather chair and directed the men to the office. She opened the door and led the men into the tidy office.

"Sibyl, these people need help. It's an urgent situation, they have three missing children."

Detective Sibyl Castafiore was a young private investigator, yet she had years of experience. She welcomed the men and listened to their problem. Hugh and Peter sat down and began to explain everything that had happened over the past days.

"You came to the right place for help. I will contact my colleagues and we will search the Citadel of Qaitbay."

"Thank you so much," Hugh replied.

"We need to go there ourselves. There's no time to waste," Detective Xavier said.

The two detectives and men rushed out of the office and outside the police station. They walked to Detective Sibyl's Volkswagen hatchback and got in. Within seconds the engine revived and roared as the hatchback reversed and headed for the Citadel.

A few miles south of the police station, Ethan Dunn's phone beeped. He opened the e-mail from Hugh and read it.

Ethan,
Meet me in the Citadel of Qaitbay.
Hugh.

"Land near the Citadel of Qaitbay," Ethan told the pilot.

The black Eurocopter EC130 helicopter gained speed as it headed to the Citadel of Qaitbay.

Joan slowly opened her eyes. There was a deafening sound, much like the fierce roar of a helicopter. She was sitting beside Tom Wood. In front of her were two people; Andrew Wood who was the pilot and Ethan Dunn. As Joan shifted, she found herself facing the window, surrounded by endless blue sky. Looking down, a city lay before her. Amid a contour of buildings and roads, a single facade dominated Joan's field of view. She sat bolt upright in bed, pain exploding in her head. She fought off the searing throb and fixed her gaze on the tower.

Joan knew the medieval structure well.

Unfortunately, it was also located 130 miles from Cairo.

TWENTY-TWO

Larry inserted the key into the metal keyhole. He turned the key and could hear the faint clicking sound of a lock. He then took out the key and waited. Nothing. Then he pushed against the wall, revealing a hidden room beyond. Larry and James were bewildered at what they saw in front of them – piles of shimmering gold as high as the ceiling.

"James, we found it!" Larry said excitedly.

"The lost treasure! And is that Alexander's sarcophagus I can see?"

"It is!" Larry exclaimed.

"James, we can save your sister. Call your father."

James took out his phone and began to call his father to tell him the news. But his attempt failed as there was no signal in the underground room. He climbed back up to the surface. He tried again but the signal was weak. Outside into the hot summer afternoon he tried to call again.

Hugh's phone buzzed to life in his pocket. He took it out and answered.

"Hello?"

The voice on the phone was familiar. "Dad, it's me!"

"James!" Hugh shouted. Everyone in the car stared at him. "Where are you?!"

"We're alright, but we still haven't found Joan. I'm at the Citadel of Qaitbay with Larry."

"I'm on my way with Peter. Just stay put."

As James was talking he saw a familiar person in the distance. He wore black sunglasses and a black outfit – Ethan Dunn had found them.

"Dad, you better hurry up! Ethan is here!"

"What?" Hugh shouted again. Then the phone hung up. "Detective Sibyl how fast can you get there?"

"Don't worry Hugh, we are almost there," Sibyl replied. She had just taken the third exit onto El-Tahrir Square.

Ethan Dunn started running. He ran towards the fortress after seeing James. Behind him one of his men walked with Joan to make sure she did not run. He ran into the fortress but could not see James.

James jumped back in the underground room in fright.

"What is it?" Larry asked.

"It's Ethan! He's here!"

"Oh no! We have to lead him away from the treasure."

"No!" James replied sternly. "Joan matters first! We have to face him."

The boys ran into the hallway. Ethan was nowhere in sight – but there was Joan struggling against the grip of Andrew Wood.

"James! Larry!"

"Hold her tight, Andrew," Ethan said coming out from behind a pillar. He stood behind the boys. "Where's your father? I was expecting him to be here."

"He is not here," James replied. "Why don't you hand over my sister? We have what you want."

Ethan concentrated his gaze at James. "The lost treasures of Alexander the Great?"

James's mind was racing. "On the third floor, under the sultan's seat," he lied. He had to find a way to keep him occupied before his father arrived with help. "We found it at the third floor."

Larry knew the plan very well. It was a distraction.

"Show me," Ethan said sternly.

The boys led the group back into the fortress and headed straight for the stairway and away from the turret. They ascended past the first and second floors and arrived at the third floor.

"Where?" Ethan asked.

The duo turned to Joan. Larry winked at her. Joan was puzzled but in a matter of seconds understood the plan. It was a distraction. He winked again hoping she understood. As a sign showing she understood, she winked back. Larry turned to James. James was looking back at him and he winked. His mind was racing and his pulse sped up. The next seconds were a blur. Larry and James both turned and punched Ethan and Joan stepped on Andrew's foot, elbow-punching him in the chest at the same time. Their cries of agony echoed throughout the room, but the three teenagers knew they wouldn't have much of a head start to find their father. Running down the stairs, neither of them looked back. Andrew clenched his chest in agony. He rushed after the teenagers.

"Not again!"

TWENTY-THREE

With a violent surge, Andrew dashed across the hallway. The staircase came into view. He checked his weapon and bolted down the stairs. He fired into the stairs. The bullet ricocheted back off the bare floor and barely missed him. He looked down but there was no one there. The teenagers had vanished.

The footsteps were coming fast. Joan knew it was only a matter of seconds before their assailant would come running down from above. From the higher ground, the assailant would undoubtedly see them.

Footsteps now thundered above them, loud leaping footsteps rushing down the stairs. Larry could not keep on running. His muscles burned. Then he heard another gunshot from above. The gunshot urged him to keep on running down the stairs. They were approaching the first floor now. He needed a plan, but if he followed James and Joan with Andrew behind them, they would all be trapped. He swiftly turned into an alcove and stood there motionless. James and Joan were ahead of him and did not see him. A few seconds later Andrew came running down the stairs. He too did not see him. He waited for three seconds before going back down the stairs after Andrew.

Andrew finally caught up with the teenagers. They stopped and turned directly at him. He aimed directly at them but then noticed something odd. There were only two. One was missing. Suddenly, someone tackled him from behind, his gun falling to the floor. Larry and Andrew fought for the weapon, pulling each other closer to the edge of the balcony three stories above the courtyard. With one last punch, Larry grabbed the rail with his free hand and kicked Andrew square in the chest. The man stumbled and tried to find a hold on the ledge, but then his left foot felt nothing beneath him. With a cry, he lost his balance and fell.

Ethan stood up and rushed down the stairs. He took out his radio and called out to Tom.

"Get over here now!" he commanded. He turned off his radio and loaded his gun.

He shifted down the stairs and looked down. A body lay still on the floor below.

Larry looked below the ledge and saw him. Andrew was unconscious on the ground below. A fall from three stories high wasn't fatal, but would certainly cause some broken bones. Finding Joan and James once more, the three teenagers continued to search for Hugh amid the crowd of tourists, hoping to find him before Ethan did.

Tom struggled to get past the people coming in and going out of the citadel. He was just about to enter the citadel but was stopped by a voice right behind him. He turned and saw two armed police officers and two other familiar men.

TWENTY-FOUR

"Stop right there!" Detective Sibyl commanded.

She aimed her gun straight at Tom and cautiously went closer to him. Beside her, Detective Xavier also aimed his gun at him.

Tom knew he could not get out of the current situation. He was alone.

"Turn around slowly!" Detective Xavier shouted.

Tom did as he was told and felt cold handcuffs tie his hands. As he was cuffed, Hugh approached him.

"Where is my daughter Tom?"

"The last time I saw her was when she went with Ethan into the citadel."

"Why did you do this?"

Tom knew there was no point in hiding anything. "My brother and I are working with Ethan. We are treasure hunters. We all knew your discovery of the scrolls could lead us to the treasures, so we devised a plan."

"You two pretended to work with us," Peter interjected.

"Precisely," Tom continued explaining.

"One question Tom, who was behind the mummy that appeared to attack you?"

"Andrew wore the costume and pretended to attack me. I wasn't really injured. We were so close but you were too stubborn to cooperate. I thought we needed more time to get the discovery, but Ethan was impatient and kidnapped your daughter to persuade you to give him the scroll. I had no choice."

Hugh had heard enough. Just before he left Tom, Hugh summoned his energy and punched Tom right on the face.

"You're fired!"

Without wasting another second, they ran into the crowd, searching for familiar faces. Hugh missed his children – James's cheeky smile, Joan's laugh when she found his corny jokes funny. He imagined he could hear them calling his name, but surely they wouldn't be here anymore. For all he knew, they could have been on their way to Cairo or who knows where. But he could hear his name getting louder and more insistent, travelling across the courtyard. Suddenly, he spotted Joan in the distance by the north tower, followed by James and Larry.

"Peter, we found them! They're over by the tower!"

Joan ran fast into her father's arms. James was right behind him. Larry ran to his uncle's arms and hugged him.

"Joan! James! Oh my God!" Hugh said. Tears of happiness started to drop from his eyes. "I thought I lost you!"

"Larry! Don't ever run off like that!" Peter exclaimed. "I don't know what I would have told your parents."

"We are glad to see you too!" the teenagers spoke at once.

The moment of reunion was short. Ethan soon came out of the fortress and stopped. Larry saw him coming out and immediately pointed at him.

"There he is!"

Ethan took his gun from his pocket and aimed directly at the group. Terror gripped the people around the courtyard as he pointed his gun. Most screamed and started running. The two detectives aimed their guns back at Ethan.

"Put the gun down!" Detective Xavier commanded. He slowly and cautiously walked towards Ethan. "Put the gun down!" he repeated. Ethan still held the gun.

"Not this time Hugh. I've had enough of you ruining my image. This is the last time you'll beat me to a treasure."

A gunshot roared. Then another followed. Everyone

panicked.

Detective Xavier collapsed on the hot floor. He felt a searing heat on his left shoulder and blood gushed out but was still breathing. He looked forward and saw Ethan lying on the ground. He was moaning. Blood was gushing out of his thigh.

Detective Sibyl aided her fellow police officer to his feet. After assuring he was fine, she proceeded to Ethan. She reached him just before he felt his gun and kicked the gun away from him.

"Ethan Dunn, you are under arrest for the kidnapping of Joan Lawson and shooting a police officer."

TWENTY-FIVE

The teenagers led Hugh, Peter, Xavier and Sibyl to the treasure room, assured that Ethan, Tom and Andrew would be spending the next decade in a cold prison cell. The adults all stared in disbelief at the contents of the room.

"The lost treasures of Egypt!" Hugh exclaimed.

"Unbelievable!"

"I thought this was just a myth!" Peter exclaimed. "There are even the lost scrolls from the Library of Alexandria."

"Is that the lost sarcophagus of Alexander the Great?" Joan asked and pointed at it.

"It is," Larry replied.

Hugh took out his phone and inserted a number. "We have to contact the Ministry of State for Antiquities."

"No need Hugh. I already called him. The world needs to know about this," Peter said.

The pale afternoon sun dipped low over the Citadel of Qaitbay, casting long shadows across the complex.

Hugh walked slowly outside the citadel with his children beside him. He looked at the Mediterranean Sea and instantly remembered his wife. But she was gone. He was still happy because he was with his children.

"Are you guys hungry?" he asked.

"I am so hungry," Joan replied.

"I know a restaurant that serves the best seafood in Alexandria."

"That would be great. I am really hungry and my energy is drained after the events of the past days," James said.

The group boarded a bus and it sped off to the Greek Club restaurant.

TWENTY-SIX

Larry Bourne awoke with a start. He had been dreaming. He saw a dim light filtering through the tent. "Is it dawn?" he wondered.

Larry's body felt warm and deeply contented. He had slept the better part of the last two days. Sitting up slowly in his sleeping bag, he now realised what had awoken him...the thought of going back home.

Twenty minutes later, Larry stepped out of the tent with his luggage into the morning sun. His uncle helped him put the luggage in his jeep. Hugh, James and Joan stood outside the "Lobby" tent.

"Larry, this trip may not have gone the way it was planned," Hugh apologized. "I'm sorry."

"Why? It may have not gone according to plan but at least I saw some new sights. We did not plan to go to Alexandria. Or find the lost treasures of Egypt! Now that was an adventure!"

"I enjoyed your company Larry. You helped me in the time of need," James said. He handed him a small white envelope. "A souvenir."

Joan hugged him tightly. "When can I see you again?"

Larry reeled momentarily. "When? I don't know. I'm going back to Washington, but we can still write to each other."

"Great! I'll give you my e-mail address."

The time had come. Larry boarded the jeep with his uncle. The engine revved and the Peter drove away from the site. Larry looked back and saw the Pyramids of Giza slowly disappear over the horizon. Then a strange thought occurred in his mind.

"Why would the Egyptians hide the treasures in the

Citadel of Qaitbay?" Larry asked his uncle. "I thought it would be hidden in the pyramids?"

Peter thought for a while. "Well the citadel is a fortress. The Egyptians must have hid it there to protect from enemies such as the Romans. They would never have thought to look there."

"But why hide a clue to the whereabouts of the treasures in the pyramids?"

"The treasures must have been located in the pyramids before being moved secretly to the Citadel."

That was a reasonable explanation for Larry. The treasures were now well preserved by the Ministry of State for Antiquities. And Ethan Dunn was a given a ten-year sentence in the Alexandria prison.

An hour later, Larry hugged his uncle and carried his luggage inside the Cairo International Airport. He passed through the security and proceeded to board his plane. As he was about to board the Emirates A380, he looked back and could see the city from a far distance.

He smiled.

All was well.

EPILOGUE

Thirty-four thousand feet above the expanse of the Mediterranean Sea, the Emirates A380 to Washington, D.C. cruised westward through the sunlit afternoon.

On board, Larry Bourne gazed out at the expanse, lost in his thoughts of all that had happened in the last few days.

As the plane streaked west, Larry remembered the small white envelope handed to him by James. He removed it from his pocket and opened it. The envelope contained a small, ancient Egyptian gold coin. Larry examined the coin and instantly remembered the lost treasures of Egypt. A souvenir.

Larry Bourne eased back in his seat. He promised himself that he would never forget this.

www.ingramcontent.com/pod-product-compliance
Lightning Source LLC
Chambersburg PA
CBHW071841190726
48292CB00005B/1862